Heroic Dogs

ECO DOGS

by Megan Cooley Peterson

Consultant: Louise Wilson, MD
Specialist Detection Dog Handler/Trainer
Conservation K9 Consultancy

BEARPORT
PUBLISHING

Minneapolis, Minnesota

Photo credits: Cover and 1, ©slowmotiongli/iStock Photos; 2, ©Matt Benoit/Shutterstock; 3, ©Anna Aybetova/Shutterstock; 4, ©WilleeCole Photography/Shutterstock; 5, ©petesphotography/Getty Images; 6, ©Kevin Kirkman/Alamy; 7, ©Alex Zotov/Shutterstock; 8, ©Eric Isselee/Shutterstock; 9, ©Images by Dr. Alan Lipkin/Shutterstock; 10, ©Rita_Kochmarjova/Shutterstock; 11, ©Sarah M. Golonka/Alamy; 12, ©kremmedia/Shutterstock; 13, ©Jelena Safronova/Shutterstock; 14, ©Reddogs/Shutterstock; 15, ©Louise Heusinkveld/Alamy; 16, ©WildPictures/Alamy; 17, ©Jake Travers, FWC/Flickr; 18, ©Barcroft Media/Getty Images; 19, ©Gallo Images/Getty Images; 20, ©Lance Cheung/Flickr; 21, ©Bloomberg/Getty Images; 22, ©Gallo Images/Getty Images; 23, ©Kuznetsov Alexey/Shutterstock

President: Jen Jenson
Director of Product Development: Spencer Brinker
Senior Editor: Allison Juda
Associate Editor: Charly Haley
Designer: Colin O'Dea

Library of Congress Cataloging-in-Publication Data

Names: Peterson, Megan Cooley, author.
Title: Eco dogs / by Megan Cooley Peterson ; consultant : Louise Wilson, MD, Specialist Detection Dog Handler/Trainer, Conservation K9 Consultancy.
Description: Minneapolis, Minnesota : Bearport Publishing Company, [2022] | Series: Heroic dogs | Includes bibliographical references and index.
Identifiers: LCCN 2021005262 (print) | LCCN 2021005263 (ebook) | ISBN 9781636911212 (library binding) | ISBN 9781636911304 (paperback) | ISBN 9781636911397 (ebook)
Subjects: LCSH: Detector dogs--Juvenile literature. | Tracking dogs--Juvenile literature. | Dogs--Sense organs--Juvenile literature. | Wildlife conservation--Juvenile literature.
Classification: LCC SF428.75 .P48 2022 (print) | LCC SF428.75 (ebook) | DDC 636.7/0886--dc23
LC record available at https://lccn.loc.gov/2021005262
LC ebook record available at https://lccn.loc.gov/2021005263

Copyright ©2022 Bearport Publishing Company. All rights reserved. No part of this publication may be reproduced in whole or in part, stored in any retrieval system, or transmitted in any form or by any means, electronic, mechanical, photocopying, recording, or otherwise, without written permission from the publisher.

For more information, write to Bearport Publishing, 5357 Penn Avenue South, Minneapolis, MN 55419. Printed in the United States of America.

Contents

Follow Your Nose 4
Helping the Planet 6
Pick Me! 8
Eco Education 10
Dress for the Job 12
Find the Poop 14
Stop That Snake 16
Crime Stoppers 18
Suitcase Sniffers 20

Meet a Real Eco Dog 22
Glossary 23
Index 24
Read More 24
Learn More Online 24
About the Author 24

Follow Your Nose

A scientist and her helper hike through a mountain forest. They are looking for a rare type of flower. If they can find it, they can help save the **endangered** plant.

The scientist is looking with her eyes—but the four-legged helper is sniffing with its nose. It's an eco dog! Suddenly, the dog stops and stares straight ahead. The eco dog has found the flower!

The *eco* in eco dog stands for **ecology**. Ecology is the study of relationships among plants, animals, and the **environment**.

Eco dogs spend most of their time working outside.

Helping the Planet

Eco dogs are a special kind of working dog. They use their powerful noses to help scientists in many ways. In addition to searching for rare plants, these super sniffers can find **invasive** plants or animals. This helps scientists who are working to **protect** native **ecosystems** from harm.

When an eco dog finds what it is looking for, it **alerts** its **handler**. The dog might point its nose at what it has found.

Eco dogs may work in grasslands, forests, mountains, and more.

Pick Me!

What kind of pup makes a good eco dog? Above all, these special workers must have an excellent sense of smell. Dogs with a lot of energy are also good for the job. Eco dogs often need to be able to focus on a single task for a long time, so these dogs have to be ready to work. Only dogs that show promise go into training.

Sometimes, dogs rescued from shelters become eco dogs!

Eco dogs need the energy to be able to run around for hours each day.

Eco Education

Before they can work, eco dogs need to learn the right skills. Training can begin at any age, and the dogs learn the job in as little as three months. Eco dogs are taught to find a plant or animal by smelling it over and over again. Then, they can single out that scent from all of the other smells around it. These special workers also learn not to chase or bark at wildlife.

For eco dogs, training is fun! Each time they find what they are looking for, they are rewarded with treats or toys.

A dog's sense of smell is at least 10,000 times stronger than a person's. Because of this, an eco dog can sniff out plants and animals that a person can't.

Dress for the Job

Another part of training is getting used to the gear. Eco dogs usually wear collars and **harnesses** while they work. Sometimes the dogs also have **GPS** devices attached to their collars. These high-tech collars help scientists know where the dogs have searched. When an eco dog has found something, its human partner takes over and starts using their own gear!

Sometimes, eco dogs need to wear dog booties to protect their feet while they work.

GPS collars help handlers keep track of their eco dogs.

13

Find the Poop

Once it's all geared up, an eco dog is ready to work. If its job is to find animals in the wild, the work may be difficult. But an eco dog can easily sniff out what animals leave behind—their poop! Searching for **scat** can help scientists in many ways. They can often track an animal's movements by where it poops. They can also test poop to learn about an animal's health and what it eats.

Some dogs are trained to know the poop of as many as 12 kinds of animals.

Most eco dogs work on land, but some work on the water! These pups can smell whale poop in the ocean.

Stop That Snake

When do eco dogs need to track things that don't belong? Sometimes, plants or animals that aren't from an ecosystem harm or kill the native life from the area. An eco dog can help.

In Florida, pet Burmese pythons were released into the wild. The snakes were harming Everglades National Park. So, what did the park workers do? They found eco dogs to sniff out the snakes!

Eco dogs in California search for Argentine ants. This invasive **species** kills local insects.

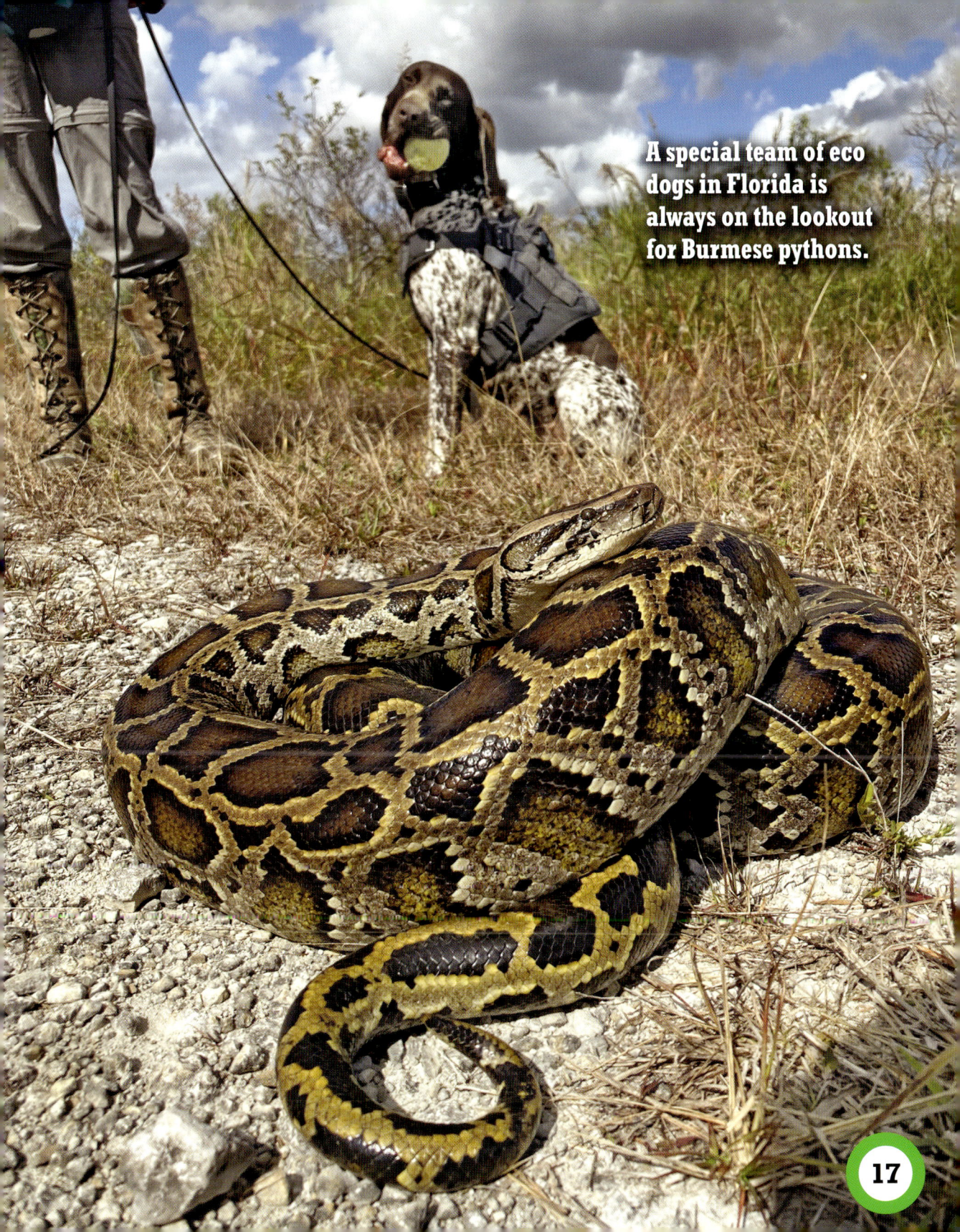

A special team of eco dogs in Florida is always on the lookout for Burmese pythons.

Crime Stoppers

Invasive species aren't the only threat to wildlife. Humans are also putting animals at risk. **Poachers** hunt animals illegally. They sell their meat, skins, and body parts.

Eco dogs help find poachers by sniffing for animal parts collected by these hunters. They can also track the animals that are in danger of being hunted. These crime-stopping dogs help scientists and park rangers keep animals safe.

Eco dogs work with park rangers. Together, they find poachers in order to stop them from harming animals.

Dogs that work to stop poaching may spend days searching an area before they pick up a scent.

Suitcase Sniffers

If a poacher tries to get away, they may not make it very far. Eco dogs work at airports, too! They sniff both suitcases and passengers to find animals or plants that may have been taken illegally. Finding these things before they get on a plane can also prevent the spread of diseases.

Beagles are one of the most common kinds of eco dogs that work at airports.

Some eco dogs that work at airports wear special vests.

Whether they're at the airport or in the field, these heroic dogs are helping to protect the environment for everyone.

21

Meet a Real Eco Dog

Russell the Belgian Malinois trained for nine months to patrol the Pilanesberg National Park in South Africa. His mission was to protect the rhinos that live there. Poachers hunt rhinos and then sell their horns.

Russell tracked poachers to help save these endangered animals. He is an eco hero.

Anti-poaching dogs like Russell learn to smell for animal parts and the weapons used by poachers.

Glossary

alerts behaves in a way to bring something to a person's attention

ecology a science related to the relationships between living things and their environments

ecosystems communities of animals and plants that depend on one another to live

endangered being in danger of dying out

environment the natural world

GPS a space-based navigation satellite system that provides accurate location information

handler a person who helps to train or manage a dog

harnesses straps with handles worn by dogs that their handler can hold

invasive spreading in a place where something doesn't belong, usually to the harm of native wildlife

poachers people who hunt animals illegally

protect to keep something safe from harm

scat poop from animals

species groups that plants and animals are divided into, according to similar characteristics

Index

airports 20–21
alerts 6, 12
Belgian shepherd 22
ecosystems 6, 16
endangered 4, 22
gear 12, 14
invasive 6, 16, 18
plants 4, 6, 10–11, 16, 20
poaching 18–20, 22
poop 14–15
scientists 4, 6, 12, 14, 18
training 8, 10, 12, 14, 18, 22

Read More

Furstinger, Nancy. *We Need African Rhinos (The Animal Files).* Lake Elmo, MN: Focus Readers, 2019.

Jones, Dale. *Search and Rescue Dogs (Heroic Dogs).* Minneapolis: Bearport Publishing, 2022.

Learn More Online

1. Go to **www.factsurfer.com**
2. Enter "**Eco Dogs**" into the search box.
3. Click on the cover of this book to see a list of websites.

About the Author

Megan Cooley Peterson is an author and editor. She grew up with two lovable dogs—a German shepherd named Sheba and a golden retriever named Gus. She lives in Minnesota with her husband and daughter.